# The Boy
# Who Became
# an Eagle

*For my family,*
*K.C.*
*For Eloise and Aldo,*
*N.M.*

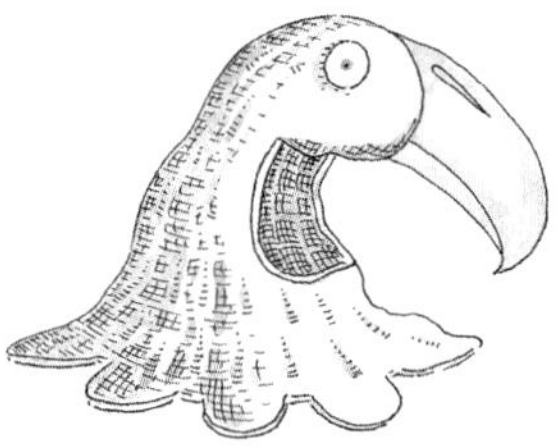

Dorling Kindersley Publishing, Inc.
95 Madison Avenue
New York, New York 10016

First American Edition, 2000



A catalog record for this book is available from the Library of Congress.

ISBN 0-7894-2666-8

Color reproduction by Dot Gradations, UK
Printed and bound in Hong Kong by L.Rex

Published simultaneously in the United Kingdom by Dorling Kindersley Limited.

2 4 6 8 10 9 7 5 3 1

The illustrations for this book were created with watercolor and ink.

# The Boy
# Who Became
# an Eagle

by Kathryn Cave
illustrated by Nick Maland

Dorling Kindersley Publishing, Inc.

There once was a boy who found out he could fly. Something told him to keep it a secret.

He got up and went home as if nothing had happened, nothing at all.

The next day he slipped off when his brothers weren't looking and climbed the high lonely path to the mountain. He ran down a slope and stumbled, stuck his arms out, and flew. Goats saw, and rabbits, but they never told anyone.

He sneaked off again a day later.
The wind smelled of far-off places and freedom.
By summer's end he could fly like a swallow. And nobody knew.

The days grew too short for the work to be finished.
More often than not, people went to bed hungry.
Winter struck like a hammer blow.

Home felt like a prison.

The boy crept out while the others were sleeping and let the wind take him high and far, to the edge of the frozen sea.

That's when it happened. Somebody saw him.

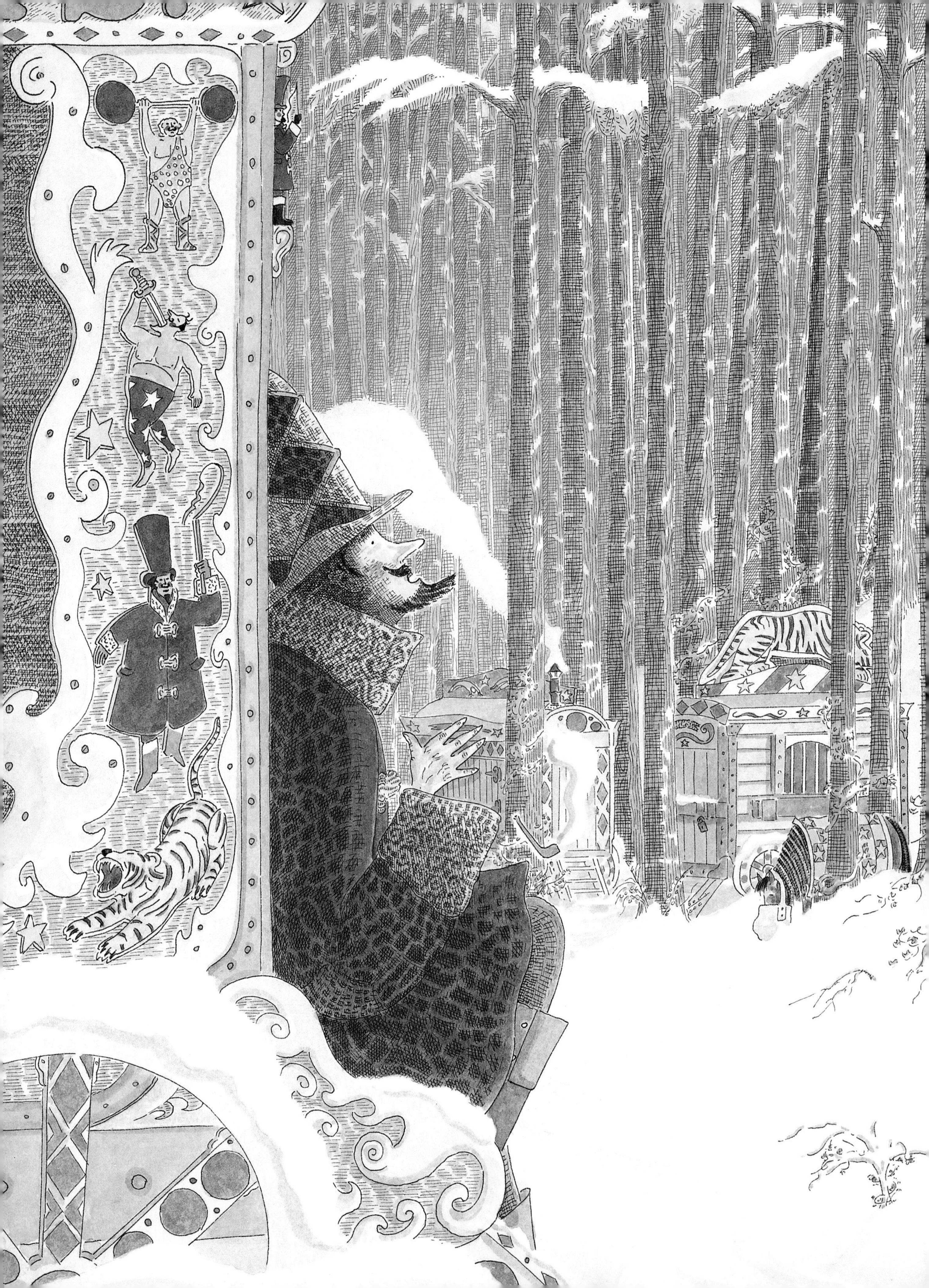

Wozzini, traveling showman, had been trapped by the blizzard with his sword swallower, his man-eating tiger, his acrobats. He called them Wozzini's Wonders, but none of them was as wonderful as the boy who lay in the snow. Wozzini laid the boy by the stove, wrapped in a blanket, and watched him all night.

When the snow had melted, the showman had a new wonder: the Eagle. The wings were Wozzini's inspiration. "Trust me," he said as he sawed and pasted. "People like a performance. You see if I'm right."

He was. Town after town, people lined up to buy tickets, and the eagle's fame spread.

All the same, something was missing.
The boy didn't know what.
One town looked much the same as another.
The faces did, too.
       Once he thought he recognized someone.
       "Father!" he cried – but it wasn't.

That evening he thought of his brothers and sisters, and the wind smelled of home.

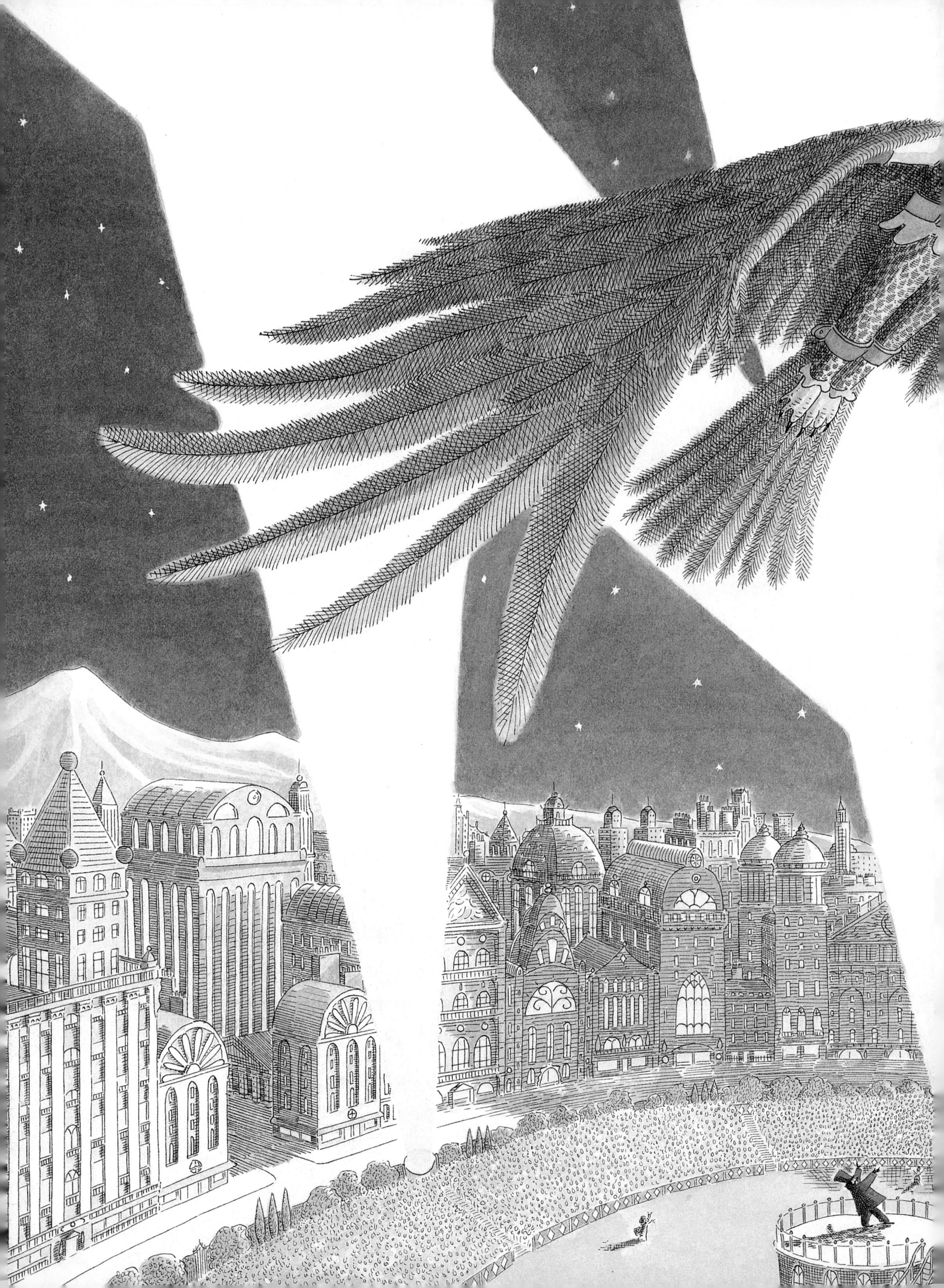

Spring came, Wozzini rented a park in the city. In a blaze of arc lights the eagle flew. He caused a sensation.

After each show the Eagle posed and signed autographs. When cash was short Wozzini let people stroke his wings for five gold coins.

At night the boy's shoulders ached. The wings were heavy and the strap around his chest rubbed a sore place that never healed.

He was tired of being famous.

Night after night he counted the stars
through the window and remembered home.

They hadn't forgotten him either. Families never forget.

One night men came to the park with axes and crowbars. They broke into the caravans and seized the wings and the Eagle. They fled to the old part of the city, where only thieves went after dark.

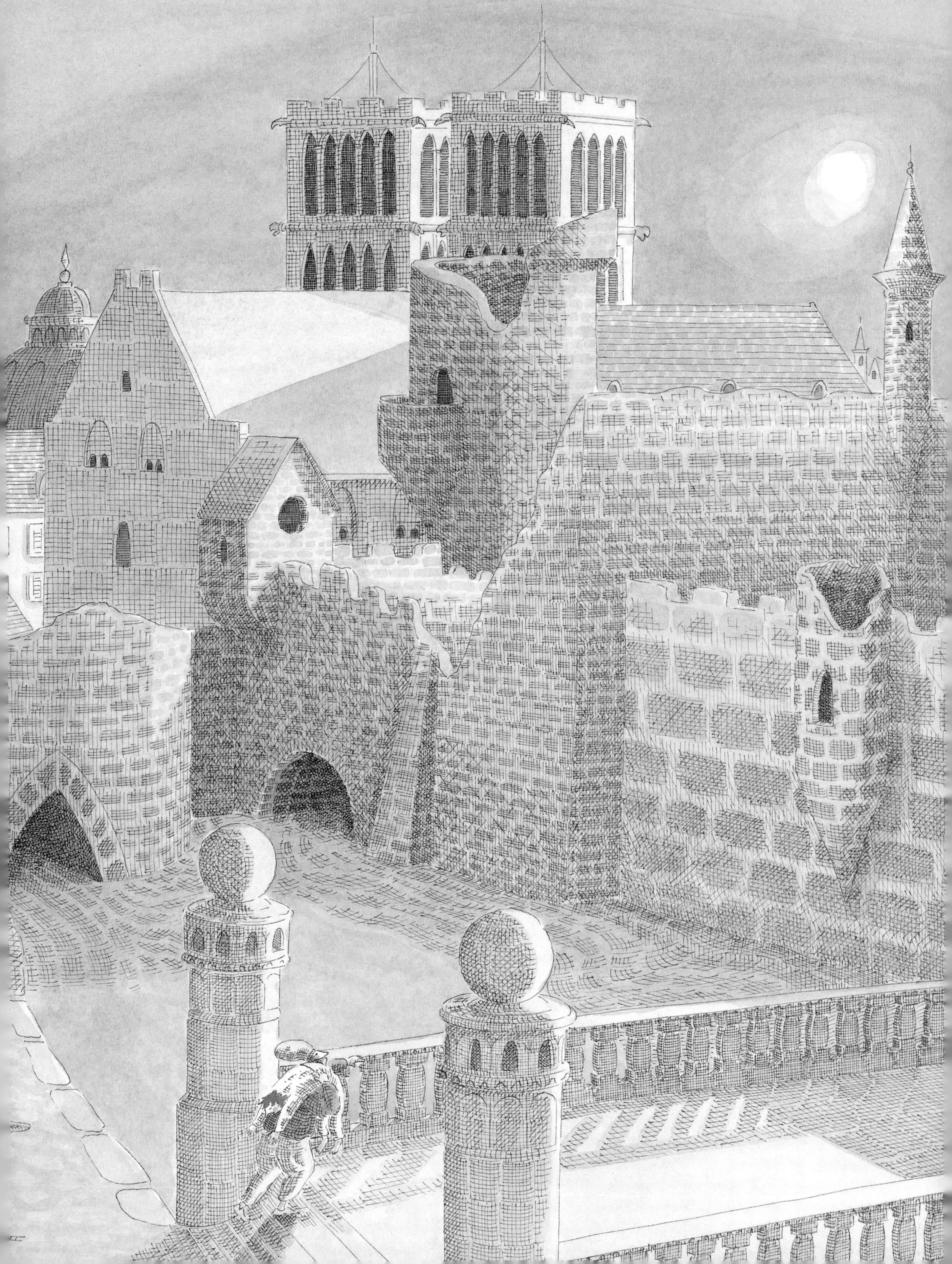

They locked the boy in the attic while they tried out
Wozzini's wings again and again and again.

When the wings didn't work, the men were angry. "Tell us the secret!" they shouted. But there was no secret to tell.

Outside the window the moon was shining. The boy had an idea. "The wings run on moonlight," he told them boldly. "Spread them out in the courtyard to soak it up. In the morning they'll fly. Throw me out the window if I'm wrong."

At dawn the townspeople marched to rescue their Eagle, but it was too late. There was no sign of the boy, and the only way out was . . . down. A robber with wings and a broken leg was dragged from the river, that's all.

The city mourned their lost Eagle.
"Poor child," they murmured in whispers.
"Did he really think he could fly?"

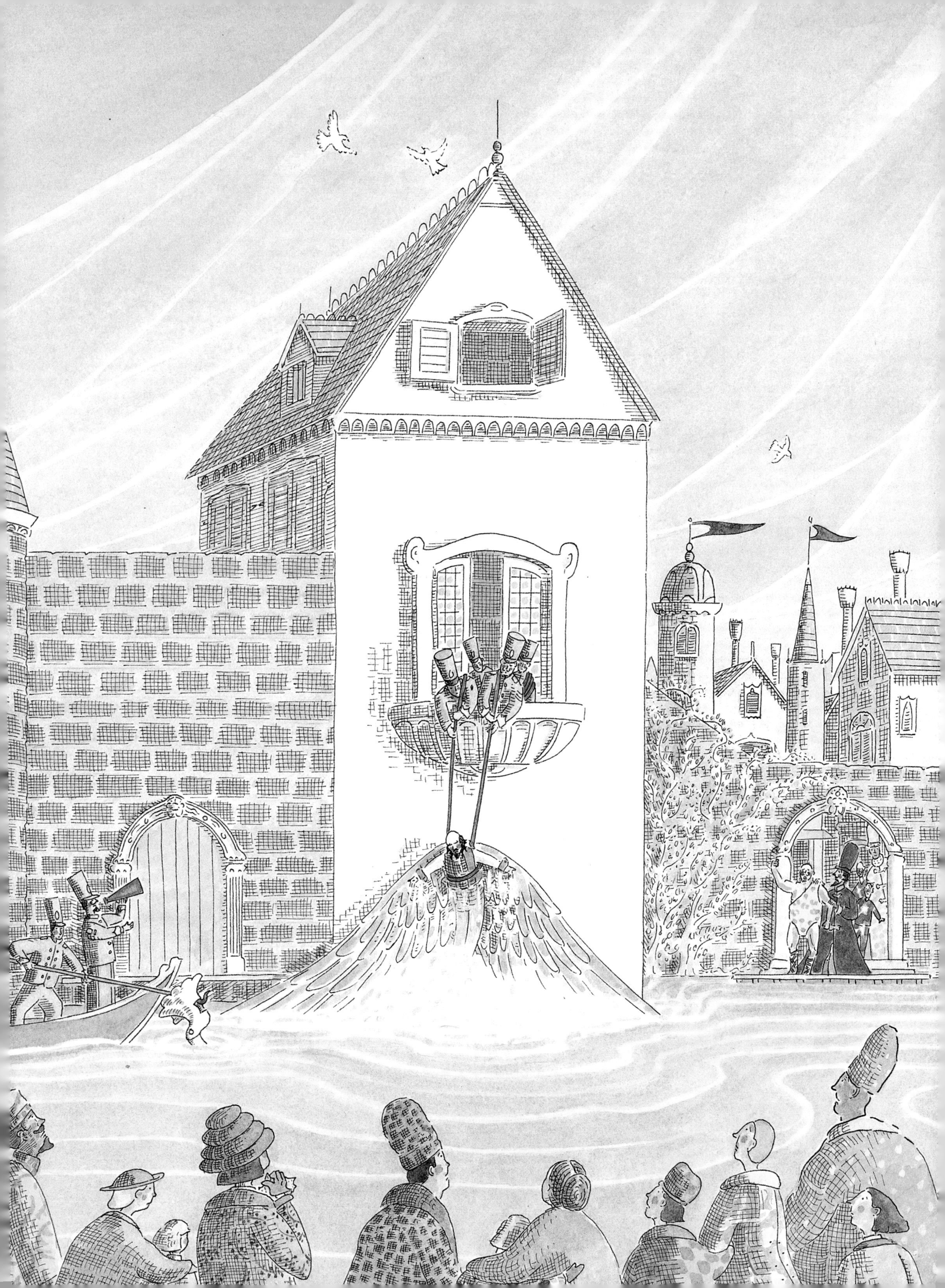

P eople came from far and wide to look at the Eagle's statue, more every year.

I come with my family. I lay a wreath at the foot of the statue
and climb to the room where the boy was held prisoner.

The wind still smells of home.